Baby Triceratops

By Beth Spanjian
Illustrated by John Butler

A GOLDEN BOOK • NEW YORK
Western Publishing Company, Inc., Racine, Wisconsin 53404

The layer of grass begins to move. Underneath, a tiny dinosaur pushes and squirms until he pries off the top of his eggshell. Out comes Baby Triceratops!

Exhausted after struggling to free himself, Baby Triceratops rests between two eggs. As he regains his strength, another egg cracks open. Then another! Before long, there are three baby dinosaurs!

Baby Triceratops pokes his head through the blanket of grass that has helped warm and hide the eggs. His mother lowers her broad, leathery head and offers food to her newly hatched babies.

After some months, Mother Triceratops nudges her babies from the nest. She knows they are ready to find food for themselves. One by one, they crawl into the tall, damp greenery.

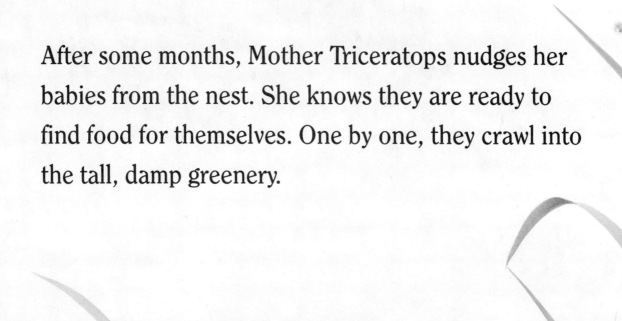

Mother Triceratops walks slowly so her little ones can keep up. Baby Triceratops watches closely as his mother thrusts her big snout into the center of a bush. Bugs scurry everywhere! Baby Triceratops stares at the tiny creatures.

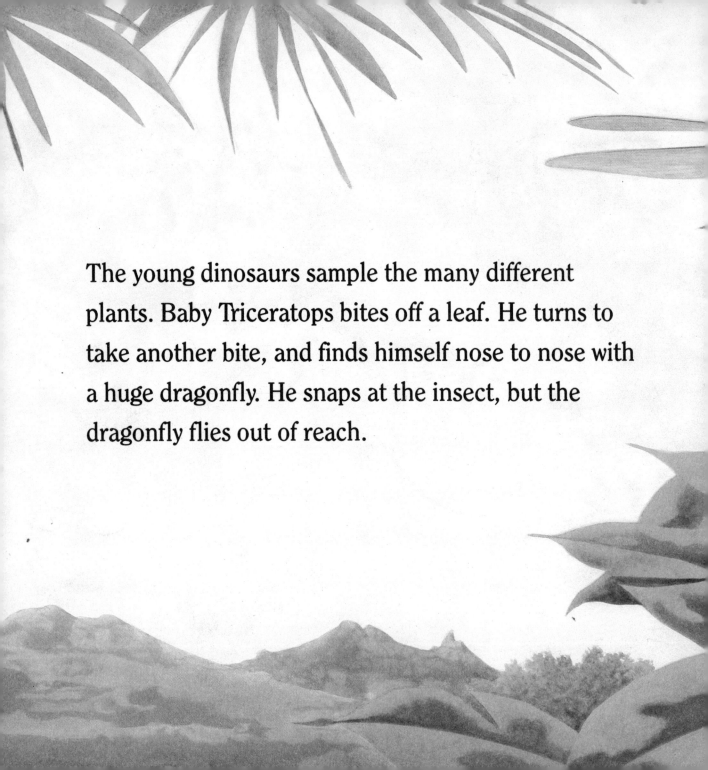

The young dinosaurs sample the many different plants. Baby Triceratops bites off a leaf. He turns to take another bite, and finds himself nose to nose with a huge dragonfly. He snaps at the insect, but the dragonfly flies out of reach.

As the little dinosaurs wander through the plants, Mother Triceratops snips off big leaves with her powerful beak. As she moves to the next tree, she lets out a low grunt. Baby Triceratops and his brothers and sisters come running.

Soon the family hears something crashing through the trees. Sensing danger, Mother Triceratops chases her young ones into the thick brush. Baby Triceratops runs and runs and doesn't stop until he bumps right into his sister. Both babies go tumbling.

Mother Triceratops turns just as a huge Tyrannosaurus bursts through the trees. Roaring and baring his teeth, the meat-eater comes toward her. Mother Triceratops charges with all her might, thrusting her horns at her attacker. Finally, Tyrannosaurus gives up the fight.

When Mother Triceratops thinks it is safe, she trots back to her youngsters. When his mother calls out, Baby Triceratops rushes out of the brush. The others are right behind him.

The Triceratops family spends the rest of the day napping and nibbling on plants. As evening draws near, Mother finds a sheltered spot beneath a huge tree for her babies. Baby Triceratops curls up next to one of his sisters and is soon fast asleep.

Facts About Baby Triceratops

When Did Triceratops Live?

Triceratops lived in North America about seventy million years ago, during the late Cretaceous Period. The rhinoceros-like triceratops belonged to a group of dinosaurs called ceratopsians, or horned dinosaurs. The ceratopsians are best known for their massive heads, horns, beak-like snouts and bony neck shields (called frills). The horned dinosaurs were some of the last, the largest and the most abundant dinosaurs. Triceratops was the last and the biggest ceratopsian.

What Did Triceratops Eat?

Triceratops was a plant-eater. It evolved with some special features that enabled it to eat tough, fibrous leaves that were too coarse for other dinosaurs. Triceratops was equipped with a strong, sharp, parrot-like beak for snipping off branches, rows of scissor-like teeth for chopping up tough plants and a huge boney frill to support powerful jaw muscles. Triceratops even had an extra long digestive tract to process this woody plant material.

How Big Was Triceratops?

Triceratops was a large, bulky dinosaur that measured about thirty feet long and weighed up to seven tons! The dinosaur was nearly ten feet tall, with a skull about seven feet long and four feet wide. Triceratops, meaning "three-horned face," got its name because of the two long horns above its eyes and a third shorter horn on its nose.

What Was A Triceratops's Family Like?

Little is known about a triceratops's family life. A baby triceratops probably hatched from an egg that was warmed by the sun or by a layer of decaying plants, which would generate heat. Scientists first believed that the three-horned dinosaur traveled alone, but now some scientists think triceratops may have roamed the uplands in herds. A baby triceratops may have even been cared for until it was large enough to keep up with the herd.

How Did Triceratops Protect Itself?

Triceratops was probably the most dangerous plant-eater of its time. Instead of running, triceratops relied on its four-foot horns and boney frill to ward off attacking meat-eaters, such as tyrannosaurus. Some scientists believe triceratops was quick on its feet and built for charging intruders with its horns, perhaps even reaching speeds of thirty miles per hour. Though triceratops lacked armor on its back and flanks, its huge frill, fringed with short, sharp spikes, protected its head and neck. If triceratops traveled in herds, the dinosaurs may have protected their young by forming a circle around them and facing outward at the attacker, much like today's musk oxen do.

Why Did Triceratops Disappear?

Paleontologists (people who study fossils) believe triceratops was one of the last dinosaurs to become extinct. Scientists can only guess why triceratops and other dinosaurs vanished sixty-five million years ago. Most believe that a huge asteroid hit the earth, causing a dust cloud so big that it blocked the sun. Without sunlight, plants died and temperatures dropped. Dinosaurs probably starved or froze to death. Nonetheless, many scientists believe the dinosaurs disappeared because of outside forces, not because they were unadapted, unintelligent monsters. After all, they ruled the earth for over one hundred thirty million years!